For my favorite kid architect, Penelope —J. F.

For Freja —Z. W.

All rights reserved. For information about permission to reproduce selections
from this book, write to trade.permissions@hmhco.com or to Permissions,
Houghton Mifflin Harcourt Publishing Company, 3 Park Avenue, 19th Floor,
New York, New York 10016.

hmhbooks.com

Design by Phil Caminiti
The illustrations in this book were created in Photoshop using digital brushes.

The text type was set in Sketch Block.
The display type was hand-lettered.

With thanks to Marc and Teddy, book lovers and truck experts.

ISBN: 978-1-328-60607-5

Manufactured in China
SCP 10 9 8 7 6 5 4 3 2 1
4500777531

LET'S BUILD

Written by **Julie M. Fenner**

Illustrated by **Zoe Waring**

Houghton Mifflin Harcourt

Boston   New York

Welcome to the critter construction crew.
Our team motto is "**Safety first!**"
Here's your hard hat to cover your noggin.

Knock on it twice before we get to work.

Hard enough? Now it's time to bring in the trucks!

Hmm. We're missing the crane. Sometimes it needs help getting into the swing of things.

Clap twice to get its attention!

Ahh, there it is. Thank you for joining us.

First, we need to knock down this building. Tall crane and its heavy wrecking ball will smash through the walls!

Point to the **green crane** and wave it over.

Swing the book left and right three times to get the wrecking ball moving. The faster you go, the more power it will have!

BOOM!

You did it!

Cough, cough.

That's a lot of dust.

Try **blowing** it away.

Much better. Now, we've got a big mess that needs to be moved.

We need the **red bulldozer**.

Bulldozer uses its metal blade
to push rubble out of the way.

Tilt the page to the right to help it along.

You solved our rubble trouble!

Ready to do some digging?

We'll need the **blue excavator** with its giant bucket and strong arm for this.

Hmm, that dirt looks hard.
Can excavator dig here?

Use your strong arm
and **scratch** the
dirt five times.

It's starting to crumble!

Keep **scratching!**

You got the scoop! But where should we put it?
Have you seen a **pink dump truck**?
Dump truck gets carried away sometimes.

Clap twice to get its attention.

Here's dump truck! Let's fill it up!

Raise the book high above your head to help excavator lift its bucket!

You did it!
But where should dump truck dump the dirt?

This looks like
a good spot.

Tilt the book to the right
to empty the dump.

Well done! Now our site is clear. Let's pour.
We need the **purple cement truck**.

Cement truck's big drum spins
to keep the cement soft.

Oh no! Our cement mixer stopped spinning. Help!

Try **shaking** the book to see if that fixes it.

That worked! The drum is spinning again.

Tilt the book to the right
to pour the cement.

Great job!

Before it hardens, how'd you like to leave your mark?

WET

Try **pressing** your hand into the cement.

Now you can say you had a hand in this project.

Let's do some planting. **Orange forklift** will move our trees for us with its metal fork.

Where should we plant them?
Tap the holes in the ground.

Looks fantastic!

You really have a green thumb.

Now there's just one last thing. Here comes the **yellow flatbed truck**.

It makes a beeping sound as it backs up.
Can you say "**beep, beep, beep**"?

All set.
We'll need the whole
crew to move this.
Show us your muscles!

Today you helped the trucks
build something really special.
Turn the page to see!

Ta-da! Thanks for giving us
a hand with this project.

Pat yourself on the back
for a job well done.